That's Papa's Way

Kate Banks   Pictures by **Lauren Castillo**

Frances Foster Books • Farrar, Straus and Giroux • New York

For Papa Pierluigi —K.B.

For Grandma and Grandpa,
who taught me how to fish —L.C.

Text copyright © 2009 by Kate Banks
Pictures copyright © 2009 by Lauren Castillo
Distributed in Canada by Douglas & McIntyre Ltd.
Printed and bound in China by South China Printing Co. Ltd.
Designed by Irene Metaxatos
First edition, 2009
1 3 5 7 9 10 8 6 4 2

www.fsgkidsbooks.com

Library of Congress Cataloging-in-Publication Data
Banks, Kate, date.
    That's Papa's way / Kate Banks ; pictures by Lauren Castillo.— 1st ed.
       p.   cm.
    Summary: When a father and child go fishing together, each does certain things his own
way, and both have a wonderful day.
    ISBN-13: 978-0-374-37445-7
    ISBN-10: 0-374-37445-7
    [1. Father and child—Fiction.   2. Fishing—Fiction.   3. Individuality—Fiction.]   I. Castillo,
Lauren, ill.   II. Title.

PZ7.B22594 Thc 2009
[E]—dc22
                                                                                        2007045475

Papa gets a coffee can and I take my shovel.

We creep into the woods. It's early morning.
The twigs snap and crackle under our feet.
We are looking for earthworms.

Papa stops and kneels down. I begin digging.
One wiggly worm curls its head out of the soil.
Then another.

Papa picks them up with his fingers
and drops them in the coffee can.
That's his way.
I scoop them up with my shovel.
That's my way.

Papa takes the oars and the fishing rods from the boathouse.

I get the life jackets.

We walk down to the shore side by side.

The sun is rising like a big yellow balloon.

The water is still.

Freshwater clams stretch open their mouths.
I find a silvery shell and show it to Papa.

Papa holds the boat while I tumble in.

He climbs aboard and begins to row.
Dip and pull, dip and pull.
He whistles with each swaying movement,
because that's Papa's way.
I sing "Whoosh" as each small wave
washes against the side of the boat.
That's my way.

In a cove at the far end of the lake, Papa draws in the oars.
He puts a worm on each of our hooks.

Papa casts his line out into the water.

I drop my line plumb with the edge of the boat.

And we wait.

We wait and we wait and we wait.

Waiting is hard. I begin tapping my feet.

"Come and get it," whispers Papa to the fish. Papa says fishing time is thinking time.

He's thinking how lucky he is to be out here on the lake, because that's his way.

I'm thinking, *When are those fish going to bite?*

Other boats drift across the water. We wave. Everyone waves back.

Papa is the first to catch a fish.
He takes it from the hook and drops it into a bucket.
"You'll get one soon," he says knowingly,
because that's Papa's way.

I look down at the water. It's rippling now like ribbon candy.
The flies buzz like little motors around the water lilies.
Pretty soon I see a fish. It's swimming my way.
It wags its tail as it circles the bait.

I hold my breath.

Pretty soon a whole school of fish are circling.
I feel a tug on my line and pull gently.
Then I reel in my line,
and a trout flip-flops into the bottom of the boat.
Papa helps me out but not too much,
because that's his way.

Papa releases the fish and drops it into the bucket.
"Good work," he says, and he pats me on the back,
because that's his way.

Papa catches another fish and I pat him on the back.

We catch five fish altogether.

Then it's time to row home.

The wind pushes us gently toward the shore.

Papa lets me row. He sits behind me, helping me pull on the oars.

A family of ducks passes, quacking noisily.

Papa quacks back, because that's his way.

I just laugh out loud.

At home everyone is waiting.

"How'd it go?" Mama wants to know.

Papa hides the catch behind his back.

"No luck today," he teases, because that's his way.

"Look," I say. I hold up my fish for everyone to see,

because that's my way.

That evening we eat fish and
blueberry pie out on the picnic table.

After dinner Papa and I sit together on the porch swing.
The bullfrogs are croaking. The swing is creaking.

"What a day," says Papa. He wraps his arms around me and hugs me, because that's his way.
"What a great day," I say, and I hug him back, because that's my way, too.

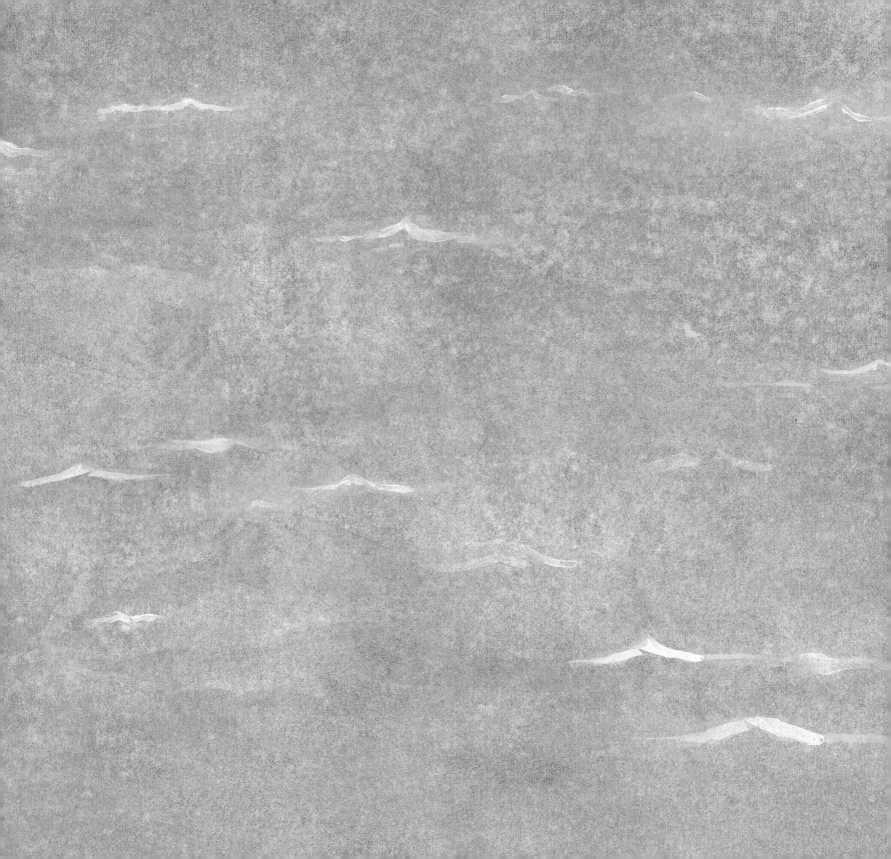